Turtle Watch

Story by Pamela Rushby
Illustrations by Cinzia Battistel

Contents

Chapter 1

Turtle Nests

Amelia and Jay had been looking forward to the summer holidays.
Their grandma and grandpa had just moved to an island, and Amelia and Jay had come to stay with them.

Grandma and Grandpa's house was on a quiet beach.

On the first morning of Amelia and Jay's visit, everyone had breakfast on the verandah. Amelia and Jay could see several people walking slowly along the beach.

One of the people pointed at a spot high on the beach. All of the others ran towards the place where she was pointing.

"What are they doing?" asked Jay.

"Ah, they're marking a green turtle's nest with a sign," said Grandpa.

"Really?" asked Amelia. "Why?"

"There is a problem with foxes," said Grandma. "People brought them here, years ago. Now, the foxes hunt native wildlife – including the baby turtles."

"Those people on the beach are volunteers," said Grandpa.
"They try to protect the baby turtles.
They put signs on the beach to show where the nests are.
Then they cover each nest with a piece of mesh,
so foxes can't dig up the eggs and eat them."

“The eggs are safe under the mesh,” said Grandma. “And the holes in the mesh are big enough for baby turtles to get through when they hatch. The trouble is, the foxes seem to know that it takes about 60 days for the eggs to hatch.”

“Often, when the hatchlings dig their way out from beneath the sand, the foxes are waiting,” said Grandpa.

“That’s terrible!” cried Jay.

"Yes," said Grandma.
"The volunteers watch the nests during the day.
But if the eggs hatch at night,
the foxes can get to the hatchlings."

Chapter 2

Jay's Idea

That afternoon, on the beach,
Amelia and Jay looked for turtle nests.

"Here's a sign!" said Amelia.
"It says that these eggs might hatch in just a few days.
I hope they don't hatch at night."

Then Jay had an idea.
"Grandpa, if someone slept on the beach, in a sleeping bag, would the foxes stay away?"

"I don't know," said Grandpa. "Let's ask these volunteers."

Jay told his idea to the group of people on the beach.

“That might work,” said Jim, one of the volunteers. “If foxes smell humans near a nest, they’ll stay away. We just need to find some people who’ll come and sleep on the beach.”

“We will!” cried Amelia and Jay, looking hopefully at their grandparents.

“We’d like to do it, too,” said Annie and Ted, two of the other volunteers.

Chapter 3

On the Beach

A few nights later, Amelia, Jay, Grandma and Grandpa set up camp with Annie and Ted near the nest.

They sang songs and told stories, then curled up in their sleeping bags.

No foxes came near the nest. But … the turtle eggs didn't hatch.

"There are no baby turtles!" said Jay, in the morning. "What will we do now?"

"Wait!" said Amelia. "Look!"

The sand on top of the turtle’s nest was moving.
Amelia and Jay stared in amazement.

The sand moved again. A tiny turtle’s head popped up.
Then another, and another, and another.
The hatchlings scrambled out
and dashed in the direction of the sea.

Chapter 4

Out to Sea

"Walk beside the hatchlings,"
said Annie to Amelia and Jay.
"Keep the greedy birds away."

They walked slowly alongside the hatchlings
to the water's edge.

A wave washed in, and suddenly
the hatchlings were swimming out to sea, and away.

"Where do they go?" asked Jay.

"No one knows," said Ted.
"They stay away for years and years."

"But one day, in about 30 years,
the female turtles will come back to lay their eggs
on this very same beach," said Annie.

"Maybe we'll come back in 30 years and see them,"
said Jay, smiling.

Amelia hugged Grandma and Grandpa.
"But we're coming back to see you long before that, Grandma and Grandpa," she said.

"Yes," said Jay. "We'll be back next summer!"